Pass Over

by Antoinette Nwandu

SAMUELFRENCH.COM   SAMUELFRENCH.CO.UK

FOR PRODUCTION ENQUIRIES

UNITED STATES AND CANADA
Info@SamuelFrench.com
1-866-598-8449

UNITED KINGDOM AND EUROPE
Plays@SamuelFrench.co.uk
020-7255-4302

Each title is subject to availability from Samuel French, depending upon country of performance. Please be aware that *PASS OVER* may not be licensed by Samuel French in your territory. Professional and amateur producers should contact the nearest Samuel French office or licensing partner to verify availability.

MUSIC USE NOTE

Licensees are solely responsible for obtaining formal written permission from copyright owners to use copyrighted music in the performance of this play and are strongly cautioned to do so. If no such permission is obtained by the licensee, then the licensee must use only original music that the licensee owns and controls. Licensees are solely responsible and liable for all music clearances and shall indemnify the copyright owners of the play(s) and their licensing agent, Samuel French, against any costs, expenses, losses and liabilities arising from the use of music by licensees. Please contact the appropriate music licensing authority in your territory for the rights to any incidental music.

IMPORTANT BILLING AND CREDIT REQUIREMENTS

If you have obtained performance rights to this title, please refer to your licensing agreement for important billing and credit requirements.

PASS OVER was first produced by Steppenwolf Theatre in the Upstairs Theatre on June 11, 2017. The play was directed by Danya Taymor, with sets by Wilson Chin, costumes by Dede M. Ayite, lighting by Marcus Doshi, sound by Ray Nardelli, and fight direction by Matt Hawkins. The cast was as follows:

MOSES .... John Michael Hill
KITCH ....Julian Parker
MISTER / OSSIFER............................... Ryan Hallahan

PASS OVER was subsequently produced by Lincoln Center Theater in the Claire Tow Theater on July 18, 2018. The play was directed by Danya Taymor, with sets by Wilson Chin, costumes by Sarafina Bush, lighting by Marcus Doshi, sound by Justin Ellington, and fight direction by J. David Brimmer. The cast was as follows:

MOSES .... John Michael Hill
KITCH .... Namir Smallwood
MISTER / OSSIFER............................... Gabriel Ebert

CHARACTERS

MOSES – black, male, late teens/early twenties. a young man from the ghetto. brokenhearted. courageous. angry. sad

but also a slave driver

but also the prophesied leader of God's chosen people

KITCH – black, male, late teens/early twenties. a young man from the ghetto and Moses' best friend. jovial. loyal. kind. naïve. a lovely friend to have

but also a slave

but also one of God's chosen

MISTER – white, male, late twenties/early thirties. a man in a light-colored suit. out of his element. earnest. wholesome. terrified

but also a plantation owner

but also pharaoh's son

OSSIFER – white, male, late twenties/early thirties. an enforcer of the law. not from around here, but always around. pragmatic. intimidating. also terrified. the actor playing Mister should also play Ossifer

but also a patroller

but also a soldier in pharaoh's army

SETTING

now. right now
but also 1855
but also 13th century BCE

TIME

a ghetto street. a lamppost. night
but also a plantation
but also Egypt, a city built by slaves

AUTHOR'S NOTES

This play is best served when the language is unadorned with sound effects or underscoring. The words are the music. Treat them as such.

Line breaks and the absence of punctuation are an invitation to play. Don't feel the need to pause at the end of each line.

(.....) indicate an absence of dialogue, not an absence of communication.

[Bracketed] words are only given to clarify dialogue and should not be spoken.

And lastly, though a short pause is fine, this play should NOT have an intermission. If Moses and Kitch can't leave, neither can you.

A Note About the Language in this Play

Let me be crystal clear: Aside from the actors saying lines of dialogue while in character, this play is in no way shape or form an invitation for anyone to use the n-word. Not during table work, not during talkbacks, not during after-work drinks.

If you're running the room, then set the tone straight away. All you have to say is something like, when you want to talk about the n-word, say "the n-word." Everyone will know what you mean! And then make sure everyone does exactly that.

ACT ONE

(A ghetto street.)

(A lamppost.)

(Night.)

*(Two men, **MOSES** and **KITCH**, are on the block. Both wear dark-colored pants, sagging. Tanks or t-shirts. Trainers, maybe Tims. Black baseball caps, brims crisp, cocked to the side or backwards.)*

(They also have one hoodie between them, which they share.)

*(**MOSES**, who is sleeping, wears it now.)*

*(**KITCH** keeps watch.)*

*(Then **MOSES** wakes up.)*

MOSES. yo kill me now

KITCH. bang bang

MOSES. nigga

KITCH. what's good
   my nigga

MOSES. man
   you know

KITCH. you know
   i know

MOSES. you know
   i know
   you know

KITCH. you know
   i know

you know
    i know
MOSES. you know
    i know
    you know
    i know
    you know
KITCH. you know
    i know
    you know
    i know
    you know
    you i –
    you know –
    you –
    shit!
MOSES. my nigga
KITCH. shit!
MOSES. you –
    shit you –
KITCH. fuck you nigga damn
MOSES. dat shit be funny tho
KITCH. yeah man it be a'ight
MOSES. *(mocking)* you i –
    you know –
    you –
    shit
KITCH. yo moses
    they come at'chu
MOSES. da fuck you think
    man damn
KITCH. ain't let em break you tho
    i mean
    you let em break you moses

MOSES. niggaaaaa
who da fuck i be
KITCH. you moses man
you moses
MOSES. nigga damn
they bess be glad
i ain't break them
KITCH. yo dat's wassup
MOSES. ya herd

>   (**MOSES** *and* **KITCH** *give each other daps.*)

yo moses
dat's wassup

>   (**MOSES** *and* **KITCH** *flinch.*)
>   (*A moment. Silence. Stillness.*)
>   (*Then, all clear.*)

man
what'chu fixta do today
man damn
KITCH. man
i'on know man
what'chu fixta do
MOSES. got plans
you feel me
big ol plans
KITCH. got plans to stand there
stroke yo dick
MOSES. man
fuck you man
KITCH. nigga
what kinda plans *you* got
MOSES. got plans to rise up to my full potential
be all i could be
you feel me

KITCH. left
 left
 left right left
MOSES. yo fuck you nigga
 dat shit ain't funny
KITCH. yo moses man
 i thought it was
MOSES. nigga
 man i got plans
 to git my ass up off dis block
KITCH. off dis block here
MOSES. yeah nigga damn man
 i ain't stutter
KITCH. a'ight nigga damn
MOSES. a'ight
KITCH. cept
 cept
 you gittin up off dis block man
 where you goin
MOSES. yo what
KITCH. i sed my nigga
 you gittin up off dis block
 where you gon go
MOSES. kitch
KITCH. what
MOSES. dat promised land
KITCH. promised land
 nigga damn
 you mean dat penthouse suite
MOSES. yo dat's the one
KITCH. champagne on ice
MOSES. you know it
KITCH. *(as an old white lady)* hello, room service
 i'll just have two lobster rolls

MOSES. das crazy right
    mad buttah on dat shit

KITCH. champagne all cold
    and shit

MOSES. chomp chomp

KITCH. yo caviar man
    bess not forget dat caviar

MOSES. yo
    you like fish eggs

KITCH. naw my nigga
    caviar

MOSES. nigga

KITCH. what nigga damn

MOSES. man caviar is
    fish eggs

KITCH. yo what

MOSES. yeah nigga damn
    tiny ass fish eggs

KITCH. ugh

MOSES. dis nigga

KITCH. yo moses man
    i ain't know

MOSES. cud write a book wit all da shit
    yo ass don't know

KITCH. prolly be more like ten books

MOSES. yeah you right

KITCH. nigga
    promised land top ten
    go

MOSES. nigga

KITCH. come on my nigga
    less play

MOSES. man
    ain'tchu tired

KITCH. jess go
    go
MOSES. collard greens and pinto beans
KITCH. dat's two
MOSES. nigga don't play
    dat counts as one
KITCH. yo how you figure
MOSES. iss one plate uh food
KITCH. one plate uh –
MOSES. nigga
KITCH. man
    yeah a'ight
MOSES. one hot plate
    uh collard greens and pinto beans
    how reverend missus
    usedta make em
KITCH. one
MOSES. brown bunnies
KITCH. two
MOSES. my bright red superman kite
KITCH. three
MOSES. drawer full uh clean socks
KITCH. okay see
    now dat's a good one
    fo
MOSES. my brotha here wit me
    back from da dead
KITCH. five
MOSES. yo moms here too
KITCH. six
MOSES. soft sheets
    i'm sleepin on em good
KITCH. seven
MOSES. my woman next to me

she sleepin on em too

KITCH. since when you got a woman

MOSES. i don't

KITCH. but'chu sed –

MOSES. iss da promised land nigga
if i wanna woman
imma have me a woman

KITCH. okay nigga damn
jess askin if you got candidates

MOSES. man i ain't met her yet shit
but dat's a'ight
i'll know her when i see her man
bess believe

KITCH. yo moses
dat's deep
i'll. know. her. when. i. see. her.
yeah
yeah i guess i knew
rochelle was fixta be mine
first time i seent her too

MOSES. she ain'tchors kitch

KITCH. i know

MOSES. yo do you

KITCH. we git up off dis block
she fixta be mine

MOSES. ya
fixta be

KITCH. a'ight man
eight

MOSES. world peace

KITCH. nigga

MOSES. jess playin
man lemme see
dis place i seent one time

had bright red tulips in it

KITCH. nine

MOSES. me and you
wakin up in dat promised land
instead uh jess
wishin we wuz

KITCH. dat's ten

MOSES. then
dat's my list

KITCH. maaaaaan
how da fuck you spect
we fixta git up off *dis* block

MOSES. yo kitch man
first of all i ain't sed "we"

KITCH. da fuck you mean by dat

MOSES. i mean yo ass ain't comin

KITCH. what

MOSES. you ain't invited
nigga damn

KITCH. yo moses
dat's fucked up

MOSES. yo
how you figure

KITCH. i know
we ain't no kinda family
man
i know
you ain't my brotha
but
but'choo my nigga tho
you got plans
mean i got plans right wit'chu
moses
moses

    i got plans right wit'chu right

MOSES. yeah okay

KITCH. yeah okay what

MOSES. okay yo ass invited

KITCH. yesssss!!!

MOSES. yo ass gon rise up to yo full potential too
    gon git up off dis block
    matter fact
    man
    i'm gon lead you

KITCH. what

MOSES. you heard me nigga
    i'm leadin you off dis block
    man
    you remember
    dat sunday school
    ol reverend missus be like

        (as Reverend Missus)

    say i say moses
    lawd!
    i do declare
    you bout da bess lil boy
    up in dis sunday school
    you fixta live up to dat name too ain'tchu
    lead deez boys right off deez streets
    uh violence
    streets uh anger
    lead deez boys on to dat promised land

KITCH. *(gasping)* pass ovuh

MOSES. yeah nigga damn
    i feel like i cud do dis shit
    you feel me
    lead you off dis block

KITCH. amen!

MOSES. be all i cud be

KITCH. yes lawd!

MOSES. yo kitch
you wit me dawg?

KITCH. no i am not

MOSES. yo nigga damn man
what da fuck

KITCH. man
look around you man
what da fuck you fixta lead me cross
you ain't got no river

MOSES. man iss a mega-four

KITCH. uh what

MOSES. uh mega-four my nigga damn
when one thang be like somethin else
besides
don't need no river shit
you got two feet

KITCH. man my feet hurt

MOSES. man here you go

KITCH. they do my nigga shit

MOSES. man what da fuck
you scared?

KITCH. .....

MOSES. yo tell da truth dawg
is you?

KITCH. fuck you nigga
you herd they
picked off ed
tho right

MOSES. yo werd

KITCH. that's what they say

MOSES. yo
light skinded ed

or ed dat got dem dred locs

KITCH. dred locs

MOSES. yo dat nigga dead?

KITCH. po-pos smoked his ass last night

MOSES. my nigga damn man
    when it comes to killin niggas
    dem police be da angel death hisself

KITCH. yeah nigga damn they do
    and i ain't tryina catch no bullets
    feel me

MOSES. yo what
    you think i am

KITCH. well iz you

MOSES. nigga

KITCH. moses man
    dem po-lice
    come round here
    gon ask dem same two questions

        (as Ossifer)

    who are you boy
    you goin somewhere

MOSES. what

KITCH. i sed
    who are you boy
    you goin somewhere
    i see you take
    so much as one step
    off dis block
    i shoot you dead
    you hear me
    dead

MOSES. yo kitch man
    what da fuck

KITCH. what nigga damn
    yo ass know good and goddamn well
    ain't nuthin gon rile dem po-pos more
    than a nigga don't know his place
    and right now
    you and me
    nigga damn
    our place right here
MOSES. yo kitch man
    not for nuthin
    but all dat shit right there
    plantation bullshit
    feel me nigga
KITCH. do what'chu can
    what can you do
MOSES. yo i cud
    leave yo black ass here
KITCH. .....
MOSES. yeah
    ain't got nuthin to say to dat
    now do you
    ol faggot ass nigga
KITCH. you leavin
    go ahead then go
MOSES. yo what
KITCH. i sed
    you leavin me nigga
    go ahead then go

        (**MOSES** *does not go.*)

MOSES. yo kill me now
KITCH. bang bang

        (*A space of time. It's sad and tense.*)

MOSES. yo kitch

almost forgot my nigga
you hungry?

KITCH. .....

> (**MOSES** *produces pizza crust and presents it to* **KITCH.**)

MOSES. it's not delivery
its digiorno's

KITCH. no it ain't
my nigga damn

MOSES. damn nigga
domino's den shit

KITCH. yeah dat's a'ight

MOSES. man dat's a'ight?

KITCH. yeah nigga damn
iss jess a'ight

MOSES. iss pizza
nigga damn

KITCH. iss crust my nigga
damn man don't nobody eat dat crust

MOSES. i do

KITCH. bon appétit

MOSES. niggaaaaa

KITCH. what nigga damn

MOSES. man nuthin man
iss jess...

KITCH. man what

MOSES. the least thang you could do
is jess say thank you

KITCH. thank you
for dis whack ass dry ass nasty crust

MOSES. yo fuck you nigga damn
i eat dis shit my own self

KITCH. be my guest

MOSES. ol punk ass nigga

>   *(mocking)*

i'm gittin up off dis block
right wit'chu right

>   (**MOSES** *eats for a time. Then...*)

kitch

KITCH. .....

MOSES. yo kitch
come on man
you mad

KITCH. yeah man i'm mad
naw man i'm good

MOSES. my nigga

KITCH. damn man
you a trip

MOSES. yo
you iz too

KITCH. yo moses man
you want some weed

MOSES. maaaaaaaaannn

KITCH. yo
do you?

MOSES. nigga
what da fuck man damn
we gittin up off dis block
we posedta
man
we posedta rise above dat shit
be on our grind
and dat right there
man dat's some real plantation shit

>   *(longish beat)*

so where iss at?

KITCH. where wuss at nigga damn?

MOSES. dis weed you on about
   my nigga damn man
   where iss at?

KITCH. man
   i ain't got no weed

MOSES. then what'chu say you had some for

KITCH. i didn't man
   i sed you *want* some weed

MOSES. of course i want some weed
   my nigga damn
   iss weed

KITCH. too bad i ain't got none shit

MOSES. man i should fuck yur dumb ass up
   you know that

KITCH. moses man
   be cool

>   (*Throughout the following* **MOSES** *and* **KITCH**
>   *tussle in that boyhood-manhood space
>   between playing and fighting. Tickling. Titty
>   twisters. Recreating video game and WWF
>   moves, that kind of thing. It's rough but not
>   too rough.*)

MOSES. come here
   so i cud fuck yur dumb ass up
   on about some weed
   dat'chu ain't got

KITCH. i sed i'm sorry

MOSES. fuck sorry
   nigga damn
   say uncle

KITCH. auntie
   nigga

MOSES. say uncle

KITCH. grandma
    grandpa
    auntie
    best friend
    stepdad
    nigga damn
MOSES. say uncle shit
KITCH. yo
    uncle man
    goddammit
    uncle
    uncle

        (**MOSES** *lets* **KITCH** *go.*)

MOSES. yeah i thought you would
KITCH. you know dat'chu
    ain't hurt me right
MOSES. i know i cud

        (**MOSES** *and* **KITCH** *begin to tussle as before.*)
        (*But then, in the midst of that, they flinch.*)
        (*A moment. Silence. Stillness.*)
        (*Then, all clear.*)

    yo what da fuck!
KITCH. keep thinkin
    iss dem damn po-pos
MOSES. my nigga damn man
    since my brotha man –
KITCH. yo may he rest in peace
MOSES. yo thank you dawg
    man since they got him man
    all dis shit so –
    so –
KITCH. yeah i know

        (*A space of time. It's sad.*)

yo moses man
you think we fixta git up off dis block for real?

MOSES. not fixta nigga damn
we iz

KITCH. i know man damn
we *fixta* iz

MOSES. niggaaaaa

KITCH. what nigga damn
we fixta git up off dis block

MOSES. not fixta
nigga damn
we *iz* gon git up off dis block
you feel me
iz

KITCH. we is?

MOSES. we *iz*

> (**MOSES** *offers* **KITCH** *some pizza crust.*)

so what
you in my nigga

> (**KITCH** *takes the crust.*)

KITCH. yeah my nigga damn
less do dis shit right here

MOSES. yo dat's wassup

KITCH. *(old white lady)* hello room service
yes it's me again
i know i'm such a pain
but could you also send up
i don't know like caviar –

MOSES. nigga

KITCH. cristal
six bitches
oh, and fifteen bars uh gold bullion
cuz we be out dis bitch

MOSES. pass OVuh!

KITCH. pass ovUH!

MOSES. pass OVuh!

KITCH. pass ovUH!

MOSES. pass OVuh!

KITCH. pass ov–

>   (**MISTER** *enters, carrying a small picnic
>   basket. He's wearing a light-colored suit
>   and a baseball cap. He cannot speak with a
>   Southern accent.*)

MISTER. why salutations
    and good evening to you, fellas!

MOSES. yo what da fuck man

KITCH. what da fuck

MOSES. how long yur ass
    been standin there
    man damn

MISTER. i think i've startled you
    that wasn't my intention

MOSES. yo man
    you police?

MISTER. oh goodness no
    whatever gave you that idea

MOSES. white folks round dis way
    dey either po-pos or dey mormons
    yo you mormon

MISTER. goodness no
    religion
    whoa

KITCH. yo nigga damn
    cuz if you mormon
    i will tell yur ass right now
    fuck joseph smith my nigga damn
    i do not care

MISTER. i'm not a mormon
      or police
      you have my word

MOSES. man fuck yo word
      you got ID?

MISTER. i do in fact
      i do

      (**MISTER** *reaches for his ID.*)

MOSES.	**KITCH.**
man fuck ID	whoa
man keep dem hands	whoa
where i cud see dat shit	whoa
you feel me	whoa

      (**MISTER** *keeps his hands where they can see them.*)

MISTER. i take it not too many people
      wander down this way

MOSES. yo why you askin

MISTER. no reason really
      just
      just making conversation

MOSES. what'chu doin round here
      man

MISTER. well gosh
      i'm not quite sure exactly
      what i mean is
      well
      i started in a quite familiar place
      but then
      i got all turned around
      and now
      gosh golly gee
      i think i might be lost

KITCH. you got dat right

MOSES. how bout'chu
head on back the way you came
MISTER. i should do that
you're right
i will i guess
it's just
i did so want to get
where i was going
MOSES. where dat is
MISTER. what's that
KITCH. where you going
MISTER. oh
well
to my mother's house
of course
i like to bring her food sometimes
because
because she's ill you see
she's ill
and i'm her only son
yes
yes
i'm going to my mother's house
or well
i was before i got so turned around
say
say would you mind if i sat down
KITCH. yo what da fuck
MISTER. it's just that i've just been walking
all around
and gosh
my feet are tired
it's because i've got weak arches
always have
but if i sat down for a moment

i'd feel good
not good exactly
better
if i sat down for a moment
i'd feel better

KITCH. man
ain'tcho white ass
gotta couch

MISTER. no
you're right
of course
i should really be going

KITCH. a'ight then nigga
be on yo –

>   (**MOSES** *and* **KITCH** *flinch.*)
>   (**MISTER** *flinches slightly off of their flinch.*)
>   (*A moment. Silence. Stillness.*)
>   (*Then, all clear.*)

MISTER. is everything alright

MOSES. yeah man
we good

MISTER. well
are you sure

KITCH. man
mind yo goddamn bizness

MISTER. no
right
of course
it's just
it seems like
something's got you spooked

MOSES. iss dem po-pos
nigga damn

MISTER. those what

KITCH. po-lice
    white man
    po-lice

MOSES. they out here
    doin jess what they do
    killin niggas mostly

MISTER. killing
    what kind of killing

KITCH. kind dat keep uh nigga
    in line

MOSES. what nigga damn
    ain'tchu herd nuthin

MISTER. no
    i'm sorry
    no i haven't

MOSES. *(aside)* dis nigga here

MISTER. say
    it isn't safe out here
    i mean
    you fellas should do something
    call the poli–
    or
    or i don't know *do* something

MOSES. same shit
    my nigga
    jess da day dat's changed

MISTER. but aren't you scared

MOSES & KITCH. .....

MISTER. if i were in your shoes
    gosh
    i'd be terrified

        (then)

    say
    you fellas aren't hungry

are you

MOSES.   **KITCH.**

why you askin   yeeeeeessss

MISTER. well gosh

it's just so late

i can't imagine

that i'll get to mother's now

and well

i've got this basket

full of food

good food

it'd be a shame

to let it go to waste

MOSES. naw man

we cool

KITCH. we iz

MOSES. yeah nigga

we iz

ain't on no charity game

feel me

MISTER. no

right

of course

i'm not implying that you –

gosh

i mean

i feel like

i'm the one

who needs *your* help

what with my aching arches

and this basket full of food

that i can't finish

by myself

but no

the last thing
that i'd want to do
is be some kind of nuisance
gosh
the last thing
that i'd want to do
is be some kind of pain
if i troubled you
either of you
at all
i'm awfully
awfully –
gosh
i should go
yes
i'll go this very instant
and
how about
i leave this food here anyway
yes
i'll just leave it here
and what you do
or don't do with it
gosh golly gee
that's up to you
there's cold stuff in there
hot stuff too
so
if you do eat some
don't wait too long

KITCH. what kinda hot food

MISTER. what's that now

MOSES. nuthin man
we good

    hope you find yur momma
    bye

MISTER. what about your friend

MOSES. i sed
    we good

MISTER. *(to* **KITCH***)* gosh
    does he ever let you
    speak for yourself

KITCH. yo what

MISTER. oh nothing

        (A moment.)

        *(***MISTER*** begins to go, but then...)*

KITCH. *(to* **MISTER***)* man
    yo feet really hurt

MISTER. weak arches
    it's the pits

KITCH. a'ight then
    we fixta let'chu sit down okay
    but first
    lemme ask you dis

MISTER. yes
    of course

KITCH. yo ass ain't here
    to smoke us
    iz you

MOSES. kill me now

KITCH. bang bang

MISTER. i'm sorry
    i don't understand

KITCH. did you come out here
    to kill
    me and my friend

MISTER. what a question

MOSES. dat ain't no kinda answer

MISTER. no i didn't
in fact
and please
don't think that i'm not happy
that we met
i am
i think you're both
delightful
but i told you
i was going to see my mother
if i hadn't got turned around
i wouldn't *be* out here at all

KITCH. man iss cool
sit down
rest'cho feet and shit

MOSES. yo kitch

KITCH. what nigga
we don't own deez streets

> *(A moment.)*
>
> (**MISTER** *looks at* **MOSES**.)
>
> (**MOSES** *communicates "I'll allow it" with the smallest possible gesture.)*

MISTER. why
thank you
thank you both
that's awfully –
gosh
that's awfully –

> (**MISTER** *opens the basket and removes a red and white checkered tablecloth which he spreads on the ground.)*
>
> *(Then he sits, takes off his hat, and fans his face.)*

(This should take a while.)
that does feel good
to take the load off
i mean
gosh
my feet are tired
though
i do suppose
that's what you get
when you intend
to get to mother's house
but somehow find yourself
(he looks around)
well here
i guess
you find yourself
right here
and yes
you're right
she will be disappointed
mother will
she was so looking forward to –
i *am* her only son
you see
and i was headed to her house
i told her i would come
but well
the thing is
i got lost
you see
i got all turned around
but yes
she will be disappointed
all the sa–

KITCH. yo man
    good for you
    so uh
    about dat food
MOSES. ain't gotta beg
    nigga damn
KITCH. like you ain't hungry
MISTER. what's that
KITCH. food
    nigga damn
    what kind
MISTER. oh yes
    the food
    well now
    let me see
    what do we have here

        (taking out each dish)

    we have some cold cuts
    mother does love her cold cuts
    string beans
    apple pie
    ice cream
    strawberries
    blueberries
    blackberries
    goji berries
    hm
    i don't know what those are
    turkey legs
    chicken legs
    chicken à la king
    oooh
    pudding
    beer and wine

water too
cuz mother doesn't drink
hot dogs
hamburgers
fresh roasted peanuts
dim sum
why the hell not
and last but not least
collard greens and pinto beans

KITCH. yo moses
dat's yo favorite

MOSES. .....

MISTER. what's that now
your favorite
gosh golly gee
mine too
cook the collards down
in fatback
add a pinch of sugar
that's how mother does it anyway
or was it
mother's favorite hired woman
i can't remember
well
no matter

KITCH. so

MISTER. so what

KITCH. can we like
can we get some man

MISTER. please
help yourselves
dig in

KITCH. yo
dat's wassup

>   (**KITCH** *sits down and digs in.*)

>   (**MOSES** *does not.*)

KITCH. yooo nigga damn
      dis shit right here
      wooooo
      dis hits da spot

>   (*noticing that* **MOSES** *hasn't eaten*)

      what da fuck nigga
      chomp chomp

MOSES. .....

MISTER. golly gee
      where are my manners

>   (**MISTER** *offers the plate of collard greens and*
>   *pinto beans to* **MOSES**.)

>   (**MOSES** *smells the food.*)

MOSES. shit

>   (**MISTER** *offers* **MOSES** *a fork.*)

MISTER. go ahead
      take a bite

>   (*A moment.*)

>   (*Then* **MOSES** *accepts both food and fork.*)

MISTER. give it here
      man damn

>   (**MOSES** *considers the food.*)

>   (**MOSES** *takes a bite.*)

MOSES. shit
      dat's so fuckin good

MISTER. i'm glad you like it

KITCH. nigga damn man
      where you procure
      all dis food

MISTER. i grow it

KITCH. yo like organic
   das wassup

     (They eat.)
     (And eat.)
     (And eat.)
     (It's amazing.)

MOSES. yo mister
   yo –

MISTER. master

     *(**MOSES** and **KITCH** stop eating.)*

MOSES. what

MISTER. master
   my name is master

KITCH. what da fuck

MISTER. what

KITCH. what da fuck

MISTER. why
   what's the proble–
   oh
   oh right
   i see
   gosh that's –
   gosh
   i've never –
   gosh
   i've never heard it
   quite like *that* before
   how awkward
   that's so awkward
   gosh
   it's just a name
   a family name
   so

you know
pass it down
and pass it down
i hope that you don't think –
i've never –
i *would* never –
gosh
it's just a name
it doesn't mean a thing

MOSES. means somethin to me

MISTER. well okay
what's your name

KITCH. who me

MISTER. yes
of course

KITCH. oh
yeah
okay
my real name percy
but dat's awful
so
so most folks call me kitch

MISTER. kitch

KITCH. yeah
kitch

MISTER. *(to* **MOSES***)* and you are

(**MOSES** *puts the plate down.)*

MOSES. nigga

MISTER. your name is –

KITCH. naw man naw
he moses
feel me moses

MISTER. moses
golly gee

now there's a name

(clearing his throat; singing)

LET MY PEOPLE GOOOOOOOO

(then, fishing for a compliment)

eh

eh

MOSES. man

i thought'chu sed

you wudn't religious

MISTER. i'm not anymore

but as a child

well

as a child –

MOSES. yeah man

whatever

*(**MOSES** retreats.)*

MISTER. kitch

have i done something wrong

KITCH. naw man

you good

MISTER. are you sure

moses seems upset

KITCH. i mean

he dealin wit shit

but damn man

dat's jess life

MISTER. yes well

as his brother

i guess you'd know

KITCH. oh naw man

moses man

he ain't my –

we ain't brothas

MISTER. you're not

KITCH. naw man
    we're not

MISTER. hmm
    could have fooled me

KITCH. i mean
    don't get me wrong
    he my nigga
    you feel me

MISTER. no
    i'd rather not

KITCH. yo what

MISTER. because
    you just said –

KITCH. *(getting the joke)* niggaaaaaa

MISTER. gosh
    you really like that word

KITCH. what word is that

MISTER. the n-word

KITCH. what n-word

MISTER. that n-word

KITCH. nigga
    what n-word damn

MISTER. the n-word
    you keep saying

KITCH. damn man what da fuck
    what n-word yo ass on about
    narcotic
    nitro
    nincompoop

MISTER. the n-word
    that i'm on about is ni–

        (**MOSES** *shoots daggers at* **MISTER**.)

    nevermind

MOSES. wish a nigga wud
KITCH. oooooooohhhhhhh
    that n-word
    yeah iss a'ight
MISTER. i mean
    every sentence
    my n-word this
    my n-word that
KITCH. maaaaaan
    quit actin like
    yo ass ain't sed dat shit
MISTER. what shit
KITCH. dat n-word nigga
    nigga
    nigga
    nigga
MOSES. iss true nigga
    all white niggas
    say da n-word
MISTER. what!
MOSES. or if they don't
    bess believe
    dey want to
MISTER. first of all
    first of all
    i'm not sure
    what all white ni–
    people
    all white people
    even means
    i'm
    just
    one
    person

and second of all
second of all
i don't say that word

MOSES. but'chu want to
hunh

MISTER. no moses
i don't

MOSES. *(to* **KITCH***)* yeah he do

MISTER. no i don't

MOSES. iss cool
you wanna say
dat n-word

MISTER. no

MOSES. me and kitch
cud prolly teach you

MISTER. now look
you need to hear me on this
gosh golly
i would never
ever ever
say that word
i mean
my mother told me not to

KITCH. what da fuck
man damn
yo momma
breastfeed yo ass too

MISTER. well
no
but i do love mother

KITCH. i luv my momma too
don't mean my ass
can't say da shit
i feel like sayin feel me

MISTER. well
 maybe it should

MOSES. yo what

MISTER. now look now
 moses
 kitch
 now i've just met you fellas
 and gosh
 the last thing
 that i'd want to do is –

MOSES. great
 but wuss yo point

MISTER. well
 well
 it's just that –
 yes
 yes feelings fine
 but it's so
 i don't know
 distasteful for your –
 well for people who –
 gosh golly gee
 it's just that –
 gosh
 if i don't get to say
 the n-word
 why do you

MOSES. becuz
 my nigga damn
 iss not'chors
 you feel me
 bad or good man
 iss not'chors

MISTER. EVERYTHING'S MINE!
 nope

no of course
you're right
gosh

(checking his pocket watch)

look at the time
i really should be going
moses
kitch
did both of you
get enough to eat

MOSES. yeah man
we did

KITCH. we almost did

*(**KITCH** takes the apple pie.)*

*(**MISTER** does not notice.)*

MISTER. was everything delicious

MOSES. it was fine

MISTER. good
that's good
i'm just glad
it didn't all go to waste
gosh
i'm so glad i met
you fellas
but now
i've got to be on my way
moses
kitch

(tipping his hat with a flourish)

salutations and good evening
to you both

*(**MISTER** exits, taking the picnic basket with him.)*

MOSES. yo nigga
   you good

KITCH. yeah nigga damn

MOSES. what da fuck
   man damn

KITCH. yo what

MOSES. *(mocking* **KITCH***)* what kinda hot food

KITCH. you ate some too

MOSES. only after
   yo dumb ass
   let him sit down

KITCH. nigga
   don't act like
   you ain't glad we ate

MOSES. you right

KITCH. *(re: the apple pie)* nigga damn
   you wanna eat again

MOSES. nigga

KITCH. yo
   do you

MOSES. man
   better save dat shit

KITCH. you right

   (**KITCH** *hides the apple pie.*)

MOSES. yo
   who da fuck
   you think dat
   white dude wuz

KITCH. yo
   i'on know

MOSES. he wudn't dem
   po-pos wuz he

KITCH. he ain't talk like
   po-pos

MOSES. naw nigga damn
　　ain't act like po-pos neither
KITCH. yo moses
　　he master
　　shit
MOSES. nigga
KITCH. yo
　　he sed dat
　　i was like
　　what da fuck
MOSES. what da fuck
KITCH. what da fuck
MOSES. what da fuck
KITCH. sed he ain't
　　heard nuthin bout dem po-pos
　　shit
MOSES. yoyoyoyoyoyoyoyoyo
KITCH. what nigga shit
MOSES. dat white dude momma
　　nigga damn
　　i think i got a plan
KITCH. yo what
MOSES. dat white dude sed
　　his momma told him
　　dat n-word ain't no good
KITCH. man
　　fuck dat white dude moses
MOSES. yeah i know
　　but po-po out here
　　killin niggas right
KITCH. you right
MOSES. specially them niggas
　　dat's tryina pass ovuh
KITCH. nigga

MOSES. and you and me
    we gittin up out

KITCH. we iz

MOSES. yeah nigga damn
    we iz

KITCH. mos def

MOSES. but wit dem po-pos
    comin round here
    how da fuck we posteda do it

KITCH. yo moses
    i'on know

MOSES. iss easy nigga damn
    less give all dat shit up

KITCH. all what shit nigga

MOSES. dat n-word
    nigga

KITCH. nigga

MOSES. white nigga
    don't say it
    and po-po don't be
    killin his ass
    in cold blood

KITCH. yo nigga damn
    you right

MOSES. so maybe
    maybe
    we stop sayin dat shit
    dem po-pos do come thru
    nigga
    they ain't gon know iss us

KITCH. niggggaaaaa
    dat shit right there
    so crazy
    dat i think it jess might work

MOSES. dem po-pos come round here
  we gon be *men*
  like they ain't neva seen
KITCH. i feel you nigga damn
  but –
MOSES. yo man
  what da fuck
KITCH. yo moses
  i concur
  but what we fixta
  call ourselves now though
MOSES. i'on know
  nigga damn
KITCH. mo*ses*
MOSES. yo werd

  (**MOSES** *and* **KITCH** *think on it.*)

  we fixta call ourselves
  like dis
  like

  (*tips his hat with a Mister-like flourish*)

  salutations and good evening
  to you fellas
KITCH. what

  (*Again* **MOSES** *tips his hat with a Mister-like
  flourish.*)

MOSES. like dis like
  salutations and good evening
  to you fellas

  (*Then* **KITCH** *tips his hat.*)

KITCH. salutations and good evening
  to you fellas

  (*Then they both practice.*)

MOSES. goodness no

KITCH. oh goodness no

MOSES. well gosh

KITCH. gosh golly gee

MOSES. why
 thank you
 gosh
 that's awfully

KITCH. no
 thank you

MOSES. thank you

KITCH. thank you

MOSES. thank you

KITCH. and your name is

MOSES. i'm master

KITCH. what

MOSES. well
 i would never

KITCH. gosh
 this is so awkward

MOSES. i have never

KITCH. well

MOSES. well salutations

KITCH. yes
 good evening

MOSES. yes
 good evening
 salutations

KITCH. salutations
 and good night

   (**OSSIFER** *enters, wearing a policeman's uniform and mirrored aviator sunglasses.*)

OSSIFER. yes
 good night

and salutations
to you both

>   (**KITCH** *flinches.*)

>   (*But* **MOSES** *calms him, intent on sticking to the plan.*)

MOSES. yes
yes
salutations
and good night

OSSIFER. good night

KITCH. good night

OSSIFER. and if i may
a word of warning
dangerous fellas
on the loose around these parts
now
i'll protect you both
for sure
but
all the same
just
watch yourselves

MOSES. gosh
look at the time
we really should be going

OSSIFER. yes good night

>   (**MOSES** *and* **KITCH** *begin to get up off the block.*)

>   (*But then...*)

say
don't i know you fellas

MOSES. no

OSSIFER. you sure

you look like fellas
i might know
MOSES. you don't know us
OSSIFER. say
what's your name
MOSES. my name
OSSIFER. your name fella
what's your name
KITCH. he master nigga
shit

>   *(A moment.)*

OSSIFER. what the fuck
did you just say to me
boy

>   *(The jig is up.)*
>   (**MOSES** *and* **KITCH** *both flinch.*)

both of you
hands behind your heads

>   (**MOSES** *and* **KITCH** *both assume the position.*)

you boys must think
you're slick
trying to trip me up
like that

>   (**OSSIFER** *approaches* **MOSES**.)

and you
must think of yourself
as some kind of ringleader
some kind of alpha dog

>   *(dog barks)*

roo
roo
roo

now
we're going to do this
nice and gentle
just like we always do
who are you

MOSES. stupid
lazy
violent
thug

OSSIFER. good
that's good
and where are you going

MOSES. nowhere

>   (**KITCH** *clocks this.*)

OSSIFER. what's that nigger

MOSES. nowhere
sir

OSSIFER. alright boys
let's keep it that way

>   (**OSSIFER** *begins to exit, but then he stops and takes the apple pie.*)
>
>   (**MOSES** *and* **KITCH** *do not notice.*)
>
>   (**OSSIFER** *exits.*)
>
>   (**MOSES** *and* **KITCH** *collapse to the ground.*)
>
>   (*The sun begins to rise.*)

MOSES. man
fuck dem po-pos man

KITCH. i know

MOSES. talk shit
like they got power
ain't got no power
cept dat gun
dat fuckin badge

    man

    fuck dem fuckin po-lice

KITCH. fuckin donut chasers

MOSES. fuckin pigs

KITCH. yo moses

    dat shit

    don't change nuthin nigga

MOSES. yo

    how you figure

KITCH. cuz nigga damn man

    we still here

    sun comin up yeah

    iss a new day

    and we still on dis block

    but damn nigga

    it cud be worse

    we cud be dead

    we still here

    mean we still livin

    so tomorrow

    tomorrow

    we fixta –

MOSES. nigga

KITCH. yo moses man

    say we fixta git off dis block

MOSES. .....

KITCH. come on man

    i ain't playin

    i need this

    say we fixta –

MOSES. maaaaaaan

    we gon git up off dis block

    so fast

    iss gon be like

    iss gon be like

KITCH. speedy gonzalez

MOSES. andale
   andale

KITCH. arriba
   arriba

MOSES. like dem chosen man
   dem good book niggas

KITCH. passOVuh!

MOSES. passovUH!

KITCH. passOVuh!

   (During the following **MOSES** *gives* **KITCH** *the hoodie and puts him to bed.)*

MOSES. we gon git off dis here plantation
   git up off dis block
   then we gon walk
   walk right up to dat river
   iss gon be deep
   iss gon be wide
   and we gon stand there like
   like chosen
   like niggas dis world ain't never seen
   den dat river man
   iss gon part
   gon open up jess for us
   ain't gon need no swim trunks
   ain't gon need no boats
   jess walk on thru
   and life
   dis life right here
   ain't gon be no jail no more
   you hear me
   ain't gon be no ghetto
   no plantation
   gon be sweet

so sweet
my nigga
so pure
so sweet

KITCH. like milk and honey
nigga damn
like milk and honey

(It's daytime now.)
*(**KITCH** falls asleep.)*
*(**MOSES** keeps watch.)*

ACT TWO

(The following night, though later than Act One.)

*(**MOSES**, wearing the hoodie, sleeps as before.)*

*(**KITCH** keeps watch as before.)*

*(Then **MOSES** wakes up.)*

MOSES. yo kill me now

KITCH. bang bang

MOSES. nigga

KITCH. what's good
my nigga

MOSES. man
you know

KITCH. you know
i know

>*(**MOSES** gives **KITCH** a look that stops this game short.)*

MOSES. man
what'chu fixta do today
man damn

KITCH. man
i'on know man
what'chu fixta do

MOSES. i'on know either

KITCH. what

MOSES. sed i'on know
nigga damn

KITCH. man
quit playin

MOSES. i'm not playin
     shit

KITCH. promised land
     top ten
     go

MOSES sed
     i don't wanna
     play games now
     kitch

KITCH. a'ight then
     count for me
     i'll go

MOSES. nigga

KITCH. oh
     oh i'm sorry
     can you not count

MOSES. .....

KITCH. fuck you then
     i'll count for myself

MOSES. please don't

KITCH. *(sung in the style of the funky seventies* Sesame
     Street *pinball tune.*)*
     ONE TWO THREE
     FOUR FIVE
     SIX SEVEN EIGHT
     NINE TEN
     ELEVEN TWELVE

          (then, louder)

     ONE TWO THREE
     FOUR FIVE
     SIX SEVEN EIGHT

---

*A license to produce *Pass Over* does not include a performance license for any third-party or copyrighted music. Licensees should create an original composition or use music in the public domain. For further information, please see Music Use Note on page 3.

NINE TEN
ELEVEN TWELVE

(then, even louder)

ONE TWO THREE
FOUR FIVE
SIX SEVEN EIGHT
NINE TEN –

MOSES. a'ight nigga

stop

stop

KITCH. who me

MOSES. i play one round

then yo gon leave my ass alone

a'ight

KITCH. .....

MOSES. nigga

don't play

KITCH. a'ight man damn

ol funky ass nigga

count off

MOSES. one

KITCH. man

i ain't sed nuthin yet

MOSES. hurry up then

damn

*(**KITCH** takes his sweet precious time.)*

KITCH. uuuuuuuuuummmmmmmmmmmmm

lemme see

what do i want

what do i want

what do i wa–

MOSES. kitch

KITCH. new air jordans

not thrift store new

new new

MOSES. one

KITCH. man
i ain't finished

MOSES. .....

KITCH. so when
rochelle see me
she gon be like –

MOSES. *(as Rochelle)* uh nigga
i'm still gon pass

KITCH. nigga

MOSES. what nigga
you know i'm right

KITCH. ain't mean
you gotta ruin my list

(**MOSES** *makes a gesture that says "you right."*)
new air jordans

MOSES. one

KITCH. tickets
to da most expensive concert
dis summer

MOSES. tw–

KITCH. uh uh uh [not yet]
dat me and *rochelle* go to
on a really really wonderful
first date

MOSES. *(resisting the urge to talk shit)* two

KITCH. a fish tank
wit two sharks in it
a starfish
and a stingray

MOSES. three

KITCH. a house
to put my big ass fish tank
in

MOSES. fo

KITCH. a bright yellow ferrari

no

porsche

no

ferrari

yeah

a bright yellow ferrari f12 berlinetta

in da driveway

MOSES. nigga what

KITCH. nigga

trust

MOSES. a'ight then

five

KITCH. like three

gold chains

MOSES. six

KITCH. me and you

seein dat sunrise

wit'out dem po-pos

messin our shit up first

MOSES. seven

KITCH. and then

and then

dem po-pos

dey don't ever come back

cuz like

i don't know

like

dey guns don't work no more

like dey

(gasp)

like dey get fucked up

by god and shit

MOSES. nigga

KITCH. cuz he send down
    plagues and shit
    like
    fuck you egyptian po-pos
    here's some locusts
    and some –
    what's da other plagues

MOSES. like uh dragon
    breathin fire
    on dem po-pos

KITCH. there's a dragon
    in da bible

MOSES. yeah nigga
    in habbakkuk

KITCH. yo

MOSES. and wizards
    in isaiah

KITCH. maaaaaaan

MOSES. or was it
    talkin snakes

KITCH. okay
    i get it

MOSES. yo
    do you

KITCH. .....

MOSES. ain't sed yo list
    wudn't good or nuthin
    jess ain't real life

KITCH. iss better
    den sittin there
    feelin sorry for yo'self

MOSES. do what'chu can
    what can you do

KITCH. nigga

MOSES. yo kitch
　　you mad

KITCH. yeah man i'm mad
　　naw man i'm good

MOSES. my nigga

KITCH. yo ass a trip

MOSES. yo
　　you iz too

KITCH. yo moses man
　　you want some weed

MOSES. man
　　here you go

KITCH. yo
　　do you

MOSES. why
　　you got some kitch

KITCH. yeah nigga
　　i do

MOSES. yo what

KITCH. jess playin
　　but yo
　　we got dat pie

MOSES. nigga

KITCH. what nigga damn
　　we do

MOSES. yo
　　how you figure

KITCH. dat white dude
　　nigga
　　dat picnic

MOSES. what picnic

KITCH. yesterday
　　nigga damn

MOSES. had uh picnic
    yesterday

KITCH. what'chu
    sayin it wasn't

MOSES. sayin
    i don't really know

KITCH. cuda sworn dat shit
    was yesterday

MOSES. cuda sworn
    dat shit
    was jess a dream

KITCH. *(imitating* **MISTER***)* why salutations and good ev–

MOSES. i'm good [stop]

KITCH. you right

MOSES. what kind is it
    shit

KITCH. yo what

MOSES. dat pie
    nigga damn
    what kind

KITCH. man
    you got pie

MOSES. naw nigga
    my ass got weed

KITCH. yo what

MOSES. jess playin

KITCH. nigga

MOSES. we cud eat some
    find out dat way

KITCH. eat some what

MOSES. dat pie
    nigga damn

KITCH. less eat

(**KITCH** *approaches the place where he hid the pie in order to retrieve it.*)

MOSES. yo nigga wait

KITCH. nigga what

MOSES. you remember dat nigga
broke into dat shelter
took two loaves uh bread
and some nasty ass cheese

KITCH. i remember

MOSES. what happened

KITCH. po-pos took his ass to jail
dat nigga got
three fo years

MOSES. i herd he got six

KITCH. for two loaves uh bread
and some nasty ass cheese

MOSES. for stealin
nigga
stealin

KITCH. i ain't steal dat pie

MOSES. you ain't

(**KITCH** *retreats from the place where the pie is hidden.*)

KITCH. ain't meant to steal dat pie

MOSES. dat nigga
dat got locked up
how you think his life turn out

KITCH. i'on know

(**MOSES** *and* **KITCH** *wonder.*)

MOSES. cud *still* be locked up

KITCH. cud be dead

MOSES. nigga

(**KITCH** *looks longingly toward the pie's hiding place.*)

KITCH. on da otha hand
    cud be fine

MOSES. how you figure

KITCH. cuda got out early
    good behavior
    some shit like dat

MOSES. good behavior

KITCH. man
    i'on know

MOSES. good behavior

KITCH. or
    or
    if he is locked up
    cud be
    in one uh dem art programs
    water colors
    shit like dat

MOSES. water colors

KITCH. *(singing, from Whitney Houston's "The Greatest Love of All")*
    I BELIEVE
    THE CHILDREN ARE THE FUTURE

MOSES. yo werd
    he cud be fine

KITCH. gettin dat g-e-d
    dat bach'lers even

MOSES. dat jd-phd

KITCH. yo what dat is

MOSES. nigga

KITCH. less say he ain't tho
    less
    less say dat shit got tragic

MOSES. yo

KITCH. if it was me
    if i'm dat nigga
    dat got locked up

MOSES. all for stealin
    two loaves uh bread
    and some nasty ass cheese

KITCH. and i knew two niggas
    hungry jess like i wuz
    wit pie
    like da pie we got right now
    i'd want dem niggas to celebrate
    feel me
    i'd tell dem niggas

        (as Dat Nigga)

    life is short
    enjoy dat pie
    in my honor

MOSES. yo nigga
    you right

KITCH. so what we doin
    nigga damn

MOSES. chomp chomp

        (**KITCH** *goes to the hiding place to get the pie.*)
        (But the pie isn't there.)

KITCH. yo moses
    dat pie
    ain't here

MOSES. quit playin

KITCH. i'm not

MOSES. then where iss at

KITCH. i'on know
    nigga damn

MOSES. yo kitch
    nigga damn
    you sayin dat pie
    wus jess a joke

KITCH. naw nigga damn
    it was pie

MOSES. then where iss at

KITCH. told you nigga damn
    i'on know

MOSES. well
    where you put it

KITCH. here nigga
    here

MOSES. then where iss at

KITCH. i'on know
    nigga shit

MOSES. maybe
    it wuz jess a dream
    the american dream

KITCH. nightmare
    most likely

        (**MOSES** *and* **KITCH** *have temper tantrums.*)

MOSES. why

KITCH. why

MOSES. why

KITCH. why

MOSES. why

KITCH. why

MOSES. why

KITCH. why

MOSES. why

KITCH. why

MOSES. why

KITCH. why

*(**MOSES** and **KITCH** collapse to the ground.)*
(And lay there for as long as they need to.)
*(Then **KITCH** sits up.)*

yo moses
we still gittin off dis block tho
ain't we
live up to our full potential
get dat milk and honey

(A moment.)
*(Then **MOSES** sits up.)*

MOSES. nigga i'm startin uh think
my ass might be lactose intolerant
feel me
and dat honey
shit
dat honey fuck wit'cho glycemic index
nigga damn
KITCH. nigga
MOSES. what
nigga damn
it do
KITCH. come on my nigga
you still got heart
you moses man
you moses
MOSES. iss jess a name
nigga damn
dat shit don't mean a thang
KITCH. mean somethin to me
MOSES. nigga
KITCH. man don'tchu see
you fixta do dis shit right here
git up off dis block
pasa ovuh

nigga damn
jess like you sed we was
jess like dat reverend missus said we was

    (as Reverend Missus)

say i say moses

MOSES. here you go

KITCH. *(as Reverend Missus)* you leadin deez boys
on cross dat river now moses
sed
you leadin deez boys
on cross dat river now moses

MOSES. you finished

KITCH. man
you always was
dat reverend missus favorite
reverend too
my nigga damn
dey say dat shit to you
make all dat shit seem real

MOSES. yeah my nigga damn
but now she dead

KITCH. come on man
don't go there

MOSES. reverend
reverend missus
my brotha
dat nigga got kilt last night
nigga dat's gon git kilt tonight
yo kitch

KITCH. what nigga damn

MOSES. man
how many niggas we know been kilt

KITCH. nigga

MOSES. i'm askin my nigga

how many

KITCH. my nigga damn

yo brotha

man

yo brotha knew

dis shit right here

ain't fixta hold us back

you feel me

MOSES. we iz held back nigga

way back

KITCH. nigga

least thang you could do is try

MOSES. i have been tryin

kitch

KITCH. try one mo time

MOSES. .....

KITCH. pleeze moses

MOSES. .....

KITCH. come on man

pleeze

pleeze

MOSES. how many

KITCH. a'ight then nigga damn

yo brotha

ed from the otha night

darnell

fat jay

dat nigga roll wit jay

dumb terry

wall-eyed terry

wall-eyed terry cousin

mike dat got dat messed up knee

big mike

junior

nick
jayvon
his brotha
i ain't never know his name
c-money
julio
andre
MOSES. nigga
which andre
KITCH. my nigga both
tyleak
MOSES. okay man damn
KITCH. man i ain't finished
justin
yo dat tall dude got dat elbow rash
day-shawn
day-kwan
dat nigga martin
kev
oh shit
dat otha kev
there's more my nigga damn
i know they is

>   *(a moment)*

>   *(then up, out)*

yo reverend missus
how da fuck
you spect
we fixta git up off dis block
pass ovuh
when deez fuckin red white blues
keep passin over us
MOSES. *(also up, out)* also
we never liked yo potato salad

KITCH. yo moses
MOSES. what
   my nigga damn
KITCH. i kinda did
MOSES. naw
   my nigga damn
   no mustard
   feel me
   hold dat mustard
KITCH. yo
   you right
MOSES. yo kitch
KITCH. what nigga damn
MOSES. less say dem po-pos
   come back
   keep comin back
   you and me
   never git off dis block
   man
   what'cho ass gon do
KITCH. niggaaa
MOSES. what nigga damn
   i'm askin
KITCH. i'on know man
   take it i guess
MOSES. yeah for how long
KITCH. niggaaa
   told you i'on know
MOSES. yo kitch man
   you my nigga right
KITCH. mos def
MOSES. a'ight then nigga
   one mo try
   less do dis shit right here
   pass ovuh

KITCH. yeah my nigga
    less git up off dis block

MOSES. naw nigga
    pass ovuh

KITCH. pass ovuh

MOSES. pass ovuh

KITCH. pass ovuh

MOSES. naw nigga
    pass ovuh

KITCH. what

MOSES. you herd me
    nigga damn
    pass ovuh

      (A moment.)

KITCH. yo
    you mean

MOSES. yeah

KITCH. .....

MOSES. what nigga
    you scared

KITCH. .....

MOSES. spent
    my whole damn life thinkin
    why niggas
    so fixated on heaven
    nigga damn
    i want dat good life now
    you feel me
    now
    but i'on know man
    maybe there is
    somethin to it
    why niggas stay killin each otha
    cuz in deez red white blues

dat river don't part for niggas like us
dat river crash on us
drown us whole
we ain't chosen nigga damn
we egypt
feel me
egypt

KITCH. .....

MOSES. but i understand
if you don't –

KITCH. naw nigga damn
iss good
but what we fixta
do it with tho
ain't got no gun
really we ain't got nuthin

MOSES. we got dat rock

KITCH. yo what

MOSES. dat rock
my nigga
less jess use dat

KITCH. .....

MOSES. come on
my nigga

(**KITCH** *gets the rock and gives it to* **MOSES.**)

KITCH. a'ight then
after you

(**MOSES** *gives the rock back to* **KITCH.**)

MOSES. naw nigga
damn man
after you

(**KITCH** *gives it back to* **MOSES.**)

KITCH. man after you

MOSES. nigga

KITCH. okay nigga damn
      iss juss...

MOSES. you iz scared ain'tchu?

KITCH. yeah nigga damn
      i hit'chu wit dat rock
      den what
      you pass ovuh
      leave me here
      all by my lonesome

MOSES. shit

KITCH. yeah nigga
      ain't thought uh dat
      now did you

MOSES. no i ain't

KITCH. a'ight then
      shit

MOSES. i got it
      how bout we don't do dat whole thang
      all at once

KITCH. yo what

MOSES. i sed my nigga damn
      not all at once
      i hit'chu
      juss a little
      then when iss yo turn
      you hit me

KITCH. but juss a little

MOSES. yeah my nigga damn man
      juss a little
      dat way
      you and me
      we still

KITCH. but what if dat don't –

MOSES. percy
   man
   i believe in you
KITCH. yo werd
MOSES. yes dawg
   i do
KITCH. man
   thank you man
   i'm touched

>   (**MOSES** *offers* **KITCH** *the rock.*)

MOSES. so what
   my nigga
   you in

>   (**KITCH** *takes the rock.*)

KITCH. yeah nigga
   less do dis thang
   yo reverend missus
   git them fish eggs ready
   you hear

>   (*singing the theme song from* The Jeffersons)

   CUZ WE UH
   MOVIN ON UP
MOSES. movin on up
MOSES & KITCH. we finally got uh piece
   uh the pie
MOSES. a'ight then nigga
   less do dis shit

>   (**MOSES** *considers his immediate surroundings,
>   then kneels down facing* **KITCH.**)
>
>   (**KITCH** *picks up the rock and raises it above
>   his head.*)
>
>   (*A moment.*)

   man
   waitwaitwaitwaitwaitwaitwaitwaitwait

KITCH. nigga!

MOSES. what nigga damn

KITCH. man
　　what'chu want

MOSES. iss juss
　　i think dat i shud face dis way

KITCH. yeah nigga damn
　　dat might be better

　　　　(**MOSES** *turns to face away from* **KITCH.**)

　　　　(*A longish silent moment.*)

MOSES. yo kitch

KITCH. what nigga damn

MOSES. sorry
　　i ain't da nigga
　　you thought i was

KITCH. man
　　dis shit
　　don't change nuthin
　　feel me
　　don't change nuthin

MOSES. pass ovuh

KITCH. pass ovuh

　　　　(**KITCH** *raises the rock above his head to
　　　　strike.*)

　　　　(**OSSIFER** *clears his throat offstage.*)

　　　　(**KITCH** *hesitates.*)

　　yo moses man
　　you hear dat dawg

MOSES. yo
　　kill me now

KITCH. i can't
　　my nigga

MOSES. why not

KITCH. i think somebody here

MOSES. yo how you figure

KITCH. yo somebody here

>>> (**OSSIFER** *enters as before.*)
>>> (**KITCH** *flinches.*)

OSSIFER. you
going somewhere

>>> (**OSSIFER** *approaches* **KITCH** *and takes the rock out of his hand.*)

KITCH. no sir

>>> (**KITCH** *assumes the position.*)

MOSES. .....

>>> (*But* **MOSES** *does not. He just sits there on his knees.*)

OSSIFER. *(to* **MOSES***)* i said
you going somewhere

MOSES. .....

OSSIFER. what's the matter alpha dog
can't talk

MOSES. .....

OSSIFER. alright then boy
stand up

>>> (**MOSES** *stands up.*)

come on boy
you know the drill

>>> (**MOSES** *assumes the position.*)
>>> (**OSSIFER** *pats him down.*)

i don't know why
you boys
insist
on making me treat you
like this

what i do know is
i can't go
one
fucking
day
without problem
after problem
after problem
you boys
enjoy this shit
hey boy
don't act like
you don't hear me
i said
you / boy –

MOSES. kill me now

OSSIFER. what the fuck
did you say to me boy

MOSES. you heard me nigga

KITCH. yo moses –

OSSIFER. i say
you could talk

KITCH. no sir

>   (**OSSIFER** *takes out his baton and runs the tip
>   over* **MOSES**' *face and body. It's a threat. But
>   it's not not sexual.)*

OSSIFER. i suggest
you think about
how you talk to me boy
last thing i want
is for this to get ugly

MOSES. kill
me
now

OSSIFER. i'm the one giving orders here nigger
not you

>>>(**OSSIFER** *hits* **MOSES** *with the baton.*)

>>>(**MOSES** *falters.*)

>>>(*Then he laughs.*)

what the fuck
is so funny

MOSES. you
i'm standin here
sayin kill me
sayin i'd rather die
than put up wit'cho shit
for one mo day
but'chu won't do it
wuss da matter
you scared?

>>>(**OSSIFER** *hits* **MOSES** *again.*)

>>>(*Again* **MOSES** *falters.*)

OSSIFER. no
i'm just getting warmed up

MOSES. a'ight then nigga
no time like the present
bang bang

OSSIFER. you'd like that
wouldn't you

MOSES. you wud too
or maybe you wudn't
maybe
huntin niggas ain't fun
unless niggas run away

OSSIFER. start running
nigger
let's find out

MOSES. naw nigga
    imma make you
    do dat shit up close
    cuz where i'm standin
    my black ass dead already
    all dat's left
    is how it happens
    and who gets to bury
    dat body
    so come on nigga
    less go

OSSIFER. alright boy
    i warned you

        (**OSSIFER** *hits* **KITCH** *with the baton.*)

        (**KITCH** *falters.*)

KITCH. moses

MOSES. what *his* crime is
    breathin while black

OSSIFER. don't worry bout it nigger
    just keep those hands
    where i can see them

        (*A moment.*)

MOSES. no

        (**OSSIFER** *takes out his gun and points it*
        squarely at **MOSES**.)

OSSIFER. watch it boy

        (*The space changes.*)

        (*Then,* **MOSES** *changes too.*)

        (*Then, the plagues against* **OSSIFER** *begin.*)

MOSES. against my body
    black and free
    these weapons that you wield

have no more strength
not your gun

>(**OSSIFER** *attempts to shoot* **MOSES**, *pulling the trigger twice in rapid succession.*)
>
>*(Bang Bang.)*
>
>*(He can't.)*

OSSIFER. what the fuck

>*(Again* **OSSIFER** *pulls the trigger twice in rapid succession.)*
>
>*(Bang Bang.)*
>
>*(Again, he can't.)*

fuck that
i'm taking you in

MOSES. not your stick

>(**OSSIFER** *attempts to brandish his baton.*)
>
>*(He can't.)*

OSSIFER. what the fuck
what the fuck
what the fuck is going on
you stupid nig–

MOSES. not your words

>(**OSSIFER** *attempts to say the n-word.*)
>
>*(He can't.)*

you nig–
you nig–

>(**KITCH**, *bearing witness, lowers his hands.*)

KITCH. holy shit
you moses man
you moses

MOSES. dis shit's changin now
you feel me
now

cuz we are not
the people that'chu
think we are
not stupid
not lazy
not violent
not thug
We Are Men
Two Black Men
we standin here
and we ain't doin shit

OSSIFER. don't hurt me
i was just doing my job

MOSES. you scared

OSSIFER. i'm terrified alright
and when i see you
when i can't quite see you
then the terror only grows
please
i'll do anything
i will
just make it stop

MOSES. you want all this to stop
these plagues
dat eat'cho whole damn life like locusts
stop killing us
stop killing us
stop killing us
thus sayeth my God
STOP KILLING US
and get'cho goddamn house in order

　　　　(**MOSES** *purges the evil from* **OSSIFER**'s *body.*)
　　　　(**OSSIFER** *spews black bile from his mouth.*)
　　　　(*Then he inhales.*)

(Then he proclaims.)

OSSIFER. YOU'RE MEN!

(The plagues stop.)

you're men i say
you're men
you're men
and you are free to go

*(**OSSIFER** tries to stand up, but he can't. He's too weak.)*

*(**MOSES** helps him up.)*

*(**OSSIFER** exits.)*

(The sun begins to rise.)

MOSES. yo kitch man
you a'ight

KITCH. yeah nigga
you

MOSES. i'm good
i'm real good shit

KITCH. nigga
plagues

MOSES. i know
nigga damn

KITCH. yo
plagues

MOSES. i know

KITCH. yo reverend missus
dis nigga
called down plagues
you feel me
plagues

MOSES. yo
i ain't felt dis good since
i'on know man

           since my brotha
           was here i guess
KITCH. yo nigga damn
           yo brotha man
           he'd be buggin right now
           you feel me
           buggin
           like

                    (as Moses' brother)
           mo sed what
           mo did what
           what da fuck
           my nigga damn
           yo ass was preachin
           to dem po-pos
           spoke yo truth
           like
           like blood
           up on dem door posts
           nigga
           like blood
MOSES. po-pos ain't got nuthin on us
           we free
           oh my god
           we free
KITCH. sun comin up
           we free
MOSES. i think we jess
           self-actualized
KITCH. i think we jess
           got woke
MOSES. nigga
           i think we jess
           transcended race

KITCH. woo!

MOSES. *(singing to the tune of "Oh What A Beautiful Morning," perhaps while swinging on the base of the lamppost like Gene Kelly in* Singin' in the Rain*)*
OH WHAT A BEAUTIFUL SOMETHING
OH LA LA LA LA LA LA LAAAAAAA

KITCH. *(singing the* Mister Rogers *theme song)*
ISS SUCH A GOOD FEELIN
TO KNOW YUR ALIVE

MOSES.
ISS SUCH A HAPPY FEELIN
YOU GROWIN INSIDE

MOSES & KITCH. ba bum bum BUM BUM
la la la laaaaaaaa
(uh) (uh) (uh) (uh) *[percussive sounds]*

(They laugh.)

MOSES. yo kitch man
you my nigga

KITCH. mos def

MOSES. you gon always be
my nigga
you hear
always
but after all dis shit
right here
we been thru
man
you my brotha too
you feel me
you my brotha too

KITCH. .....

*(**KITCH** grabs **MOSES** in a bear hug. It's a startling, simple thing.)*

*(After a time, **MOSES** hugs him back.)*

KITCH. yo
    what we fixta do now
    moses

MOSES. sun comin up
    we free
    how bout we
    git up off dis block
    go git some food
    my nigga damn
    you hungry

KITCH. yo less get some ribs

>   (**MISTER** *enters, wearing the suit and hat and*
>   *carrying the picnic basket, as before.*)
>
>   (*A moment.*)

MISTER. why salutations
    and good morning to you
    fellas

MOSES. yo
    what da fuck
    man

KITCH. what da fuck

MOSES. how long yur ass
    been standin there
    man damn

MISTER. you fellas going somewhere

MOSES. what

MISTER. sure looks like
    you're going somewhere

KITCH. yeah man damn
    we goin to get some ribs
    you wanna come wit–

MISTER. who are you

MOSES. .....

MISTER. please don't make me

ask you again

> *(During the following, and at the very last moment possible, **MISTER** pulls out a gun.)*

MOSES. i'm moses
dis my brother kitch
and we gittin up off –

> *(Bang Bang.)*

> *(**MISTER** shoots **MOSES**.)*

KITCH. NO!

> *(**MOSES** falls.)*

> *(**KITCH** holds his body.)*

> *(**MISTER** puts his gun away, then addresses the audience.)*

MISTER. golly gee
did you guys hear
a fella was killed today
black fella
another black fella was killed
i should say
well
because
well gosh
it just keeps –

> *(he makes a gesture for "happening")*

which is sad
you know
so sad
but also
gosh
so darn perplexing
how does something like this keep –

> *(again, he makes the "happening" gesture)*

MISTER. gosh
   and yes
   yes there are times
   i must admit
   there are times
   that i
   i don't know
   resist
   or find myself resisting
   having to listen to
   to look at
   or acknowledge
   there are times i just don't wanna know
   you know
   because it just keeps –

      (again, he makes the "happening" gesture)
   and each time
   it makes me feel so sad
   but also helpless to
   to change
   or intervene
   or i don't know –
   but then
   you know
   there are those few [black people]
   who manage to make good
   or decent –
   i don't know
   so that's
   that's really… [heartening]
   yes
   but yes
   there are those times when i don't wanna –

      (A moment.)

(Then a big performative sigh; self-conscious without being ironic.)

(A moment.)

(Then his demeanor brightens.)

anyway...

(Blackout.)

End of Play